CHAPTER ONE

It was just like any other la y, yellow sun was up, and the drying g ıd brown. The air was thick with humidity, moving every few minutes in a swift, warm breeze. Children's laughter could be heard throughout the trees of the clustered neighborhood. One such child was young Charlie, who was outside in his plastic, green turtle sandbox, killing rubber cows with rusting metal soldiers. Usually his friend Sophia would have been over to play with him by now, just as she did every day, but this week was different. Charlie was alone, and this was not something he was used to.

For a few days he ventured outside and sat waiting for her and every day she didn't come. He hadn't even seen her in school for a while. Though he was too young to really consider why he wasn't seeing her as often as usual, he knew something wasn't right. It just wasn't like his best friend to not show up so many times in a row. He missed her, he couldn't wait to see her again and show off his soldier's sand fort. Sophia was the little red headed girl that lived through the small patch of woods along the road, and ever since they were brought into this world, eight years ago, they had been the best of friends. They did everything together. Learned how to ride a bike together, had sleepovers in their backyard with Sophia's plastic princess tent and played countless adventures in the woods; adventures that always somehow ended up with monsters stealing away Sophia, the beloved princess, and Charlie as her victorious rescuer. Their parents were good friends in high school and stayed close after graduation. The moms always had gossip or shopping and the dads always had beer, golf, and Sunday night football. At eight years old Charlie and Sophia were inseparable. Which is why Charlie was so deeply confused as to why she hadn't come over and his parents weren't telling him why either.

He'd been outside for two hours now and still no sign of her. He lay in the sandbox with his chin resting on the scratchy, plastic side, watching for her to come running across his yard like nothing was the matter. Plucking the tall grass beside the green sand turtle he watched and waited patiently. She never came, and by the time it was too dark to see across the yard, Charlie reluctantly dropped his toys and went inside, surprised to find his parents yelling back and forth about something he didn't understand. It was something about James, Sophia's dad. Charlie's mom was crying more than he'd ever seen and, as he ran halfway up the stairs to hide behind the railing and listen, he heard her screaming,

"What a scumbag! How could he do that to her? And after all these years!" More tears ran down her cheeks and she didn't even bother to wipe them away.

Something wasn't right and he hated all the yelling. His parents never yelled about anything, especially not this bad. The only reason he stayed to listen was the fact it had to do with Sophia, and he had to know why she never came to see him this week.

"Mom, where's Sophia?" Charlie said cautiously while lifting his head above the banister, giving away his hiding spot.

"Honey, go to your room." His mother said curtly, noticeably choking back her tears.

"Why didn't she come over today?" Charlie pressed, now standing tall.

"I'm so sorry Charlie, but Sophia won't be coming over anymore. I'm so sorry..." his mother managed to get out before burying her face into her trembling hands and swiftly going into the kitchen.

Confused and angry, Charlie went up the stairs and into his room. *Why wouldn't anyone tell him what was happening?* He thought to himself, as he made his way across the cluttered room. Kicking his toy truck and a stuffed dinosaur out of his way he crossed over the racetrack area rug and sat in his bed. Pressing his nose and forehead up against the cool window he wished he could see what was going on in Sophia's house. As his breath fogged up the windowpane he saw their front door swing open hard, slamming against the side of the house, and Sophia's mom came rushing out into the dim light of the porch; Sophia being dragged behind her, her little pink suitcase in tow. Charlie pulled the end of a sleeve over his little fist to wipe the window clear so he could see better and try to figure out what was going on.

He could easily see Sophia's lively red hair bouncing all around her face as she was forcedly placed in the car and buckled in. She looked just as confused as Charlie was and sat there clutching her favorite ragged doll that was missing an eye. He remembered the day she got that doll. She played with it so much and slept with it so tightly every night that the once bright, peach skin was now a muted grey.

Coming through the door with more suitcases her mom frantically threw everything in the back of their purple minivan and slammed the trunk closed. Her dad was outside now and then the yelling started again. James was trying to get to Sophia, but her mom wouldn't allow it. She just pointed her finger at him as she yelled a phrase Charlie knew he would get a timeout for saying, and she heaved Sophia's door shut. And just like that she was leaving. The old car sped away in a cloud of dust, and Charlie knew that would be the last time he saw his best friend. Or so he thought.

CHAPTER TWO

Ten years later and that day was no more than an ancient daydream to Charlie. Like the dreams where you can only remember bits and pieces but they never add up to much and you can never figure out how it even started. The only memory he had of Sophia were the pictures of them as children and the toys they used to play with that were now in cardboard boxes up in his dusty, critter infested attic. His parents never spoke a word about her family ever since she moved away so he quickly forgot about her and how close they truly were. As if she never existed outside of a fragment of a thought.

It was his first day as a senior in high school and his alarm had already been snoozed three times. By the fourth irritating ring he pushed down the off button and sluggishly rolled himself out of bed as he yawned and rubbed his eyes open. The sun was just barely seeping through his heavy black curtains and he could smell strong coffee wafting up from the kitchen downstairs. Lazily throwing on some clothes, that may or may not have been washed, he went to the bathroom to clean up a bit. His shaggy, dark brown hair was stuck in strange angles from sleep so he threw his favorite cap on, and with a shrug of his shoulders headed downstairs.

“Ready for your first day as a senior?” his mom was always in an unusually good mood for six thirty in the morning. This somehow made him bothered.

“As ready as anyone could be for a fresh new year of torture and boredom.” Charlie said sarcastically as he grabbed a plain bagel and headed out to the garage where his beat up, green jeep sat waiting for him. His jeep was a never-ending project. He was always finding something to improve or something to replace. His parents told him it was a waste of money and time, but for him it was a distraction from reality. Every morning he would come into this garage and work on his most prized possession before heading out into the world.

Looking at the dried-on clumps of mud piling up on his door he thought it was probably a good time for a car wash, but then again, it'd only get dirty a couple days later. Charlie slid into his front seat and slammed the creaking, metal door closed behind him. Pushing on the classic rock station he headed out of the cluttered garage and down to school. Charlie had always done the least possible when it came to passing a year of school. He was smart enough for it all but he just didn't care. He was too preoccupied with work and football. Although he wasn't your typical sleazy jock; He was never interested in the girls at school and that drove them insane. They loved him; he was the star of the football team and quite attractive. With his muscular, sport trained, toned body and tan olive colored skin, he could easily have been a model for a Levis jean commercial.

He just tried to get through high school without all the drama of having a girlfriend, besides the fact that none of the girls there appealed to him. They were all so pink and flashy and the only words that came out of their mouths were about shopping and how they think they're so fat. He did not want a single thing to do with any of them. He was dead set on leaving every one of them behind with the rest of this school.

Well, until he saw her, it wasn't until that first day, when he pushed the familiar metal doors open to the main lobby, and someone caught his eye. She was unmistakably a new student as he watched her search through her bag for something while looking around nervously, visibly trying to stay out of everybody's way. She had the most intense red hair he'd ever seen and something about her gave him the worst déjà vu, except it wouldn't go away. Shaking off the feelings of some strange nostalgia he kept on walking, trying to forget about her.

CHAPTER THREE

Being the new girl Sophia was horrified of being late to class. On top of everyone staring at her she couldn't seem to find her cell phone which she had thrown haphazardly into her bag in a hurry to get to her first period. She needed Lucy, her best friend from North Carolina, where she moved up from just a day ago. As the second warning bell rang she gave up on her search for the cell phone and practically jogged to her class.

As she opened the door, clearly out of breath, she tried to look collected and cool but it didn't matter. She was late, and everyone was staring at her. Maybe it didn't help that she frequently stood out from people with her strange hair and almost ghostly pale skin. Of course all the good seats were taken in the classroom so she was stuck sitting in the back next to probably the most attractive boy she had ever seen.

Typical. She thought while chewing on her bottom lip nervously.

As she settled down, and quietly put her bag down on the floor beside her, he turned her way.

"Hey, you're the new girl right? I'm Mark." He said to her, flashing his big white teeth through his perfect face. Almost too perfect. She decided he wasn't as attractive as she first thought, he looked too fake and unemotional, and that helped her relax.

"Yepp, I'm the new girl. I'm Sophia." She said carefully, with a timid smile. Her nerves were certainly getting the best of her and she desperately needed Lucy to tell her how silly she was acting. '*its only a stupid boy!*' her best friend would say, and somehow that would make Sophia calm down a little.

At the table opposite Sophia and Mark sat a bubbly blonde girl who noticed this small interaction and immediately introduced herself as Claire. She had long curly hair and Sophia could almost see her reflection in the amount of pink lip gloss that this girl had applied. She reminded Sophia of a beauty pageant girl from somewhere like Texas with the perfect platinum hair and perfect pearly white teeth, always smiling to impress the judges. Regardless of her seemingly fake personality, Sophia found that right away she clicked with Claire and Sophia was hopeful that she might have just found a new friend already. Sophia felt comfortable with Claire, probably because she reminded her of all the girls she went to school with in North Carolina. There she had been in a private school that was girls only. And the entire population of girls in that school probably had more make up on than Covergirl could keep up with. They were always so shiny and clean but they were also very harsh, snobby, and vulgar. They were the sort that had money and knew how to use that kind of power against people. A behavior that Sophia was not accustomed to no matter how many years she had been living among them. She couldn't stand to waste money the way they did and she certainly wasn't about to join their cliché just to fit in.

Thinking about her old school made her miss some of the other things North Carolina had that New Hampshire didn't. She has a lot of family down there and they were a close knit family. Always knowing each other's business, but always having each other's backs. Not to mention she managed to become the favorite in her grandfather's eyes, likely because she was the most grounded of them all. Her grandfather paid for anything she ever wanted. He bought her mom's house, which had a small guest house on the property that Sophia moved into when she turned fifteen, cars, clothes, you name it he bought it. She was spoiled rotten, but somehow it never affected her. She never ended up like the girls in the boarding school who couldn't get enough of the superficial things in life and thought they were better than everyone else in the world just because of some trust fund waiting for them to turn twenty-five. They would never have to work a day in their lives, and Sophia thought that was a down right pathetic way of life.

Lucy was the same in that way. This is probably why they were such best friends from the moment they met each other. She and Lucy would often sneak out late at night to gossip about how dumb the other girls were. Which really made them no different, but they justified it with the fact that at least their hair wasn't straight out of a box and they didn't have hissy fits when daddy wouldn't buy them a new car, or five.

"She actually started to cry when a pen marked the top of her new manicure!" Lucy would say incredulously and the girls would laugh and be thankful they didn't act as silly.

How she longed to hear from Lucy the second she got home. They had never been apart more than just a few days and now they were miles and miles apart. She hated being the new girl, hated being away from Lucy, and hated everyone staring at her.

Later in the day, Claire just so happened to be in her fifth period too, which was unbelievably comforting to Sophia. They sat next to each other, at a rather small two person table, and Claire told her all about the cute and single boys, where to sit for lunch, and all the places where people liked to hang out around town. She got a good rundown of this cold, low-spirited state, but it didn't really matter to her. She was listening to Claire but her mind was elsewhere. She wanted to be alone. By the end of the long, frustrating day Sophia had gotten over two hundred inquisitive glares and was ready to finally go home and finish unpacking her new room and be by herself.

Moving from the beautiful and bright Top Sail Island to dreary, cold New Hampshire was a nightmare. Sophia missed the warm, crisp ocean air and the way it smelled and the feeling of the sand between her toes. She very much enjoyed her life down there, but it had been three years since she last saw her father in New Hampshire and he had finally convinced her mom to let her live just one year with him. So, two days before school started she was told to pack up all her favorite things into her brand new shiny car and drive the twenty hours to her dad's new house.

So here she was, wishing the year would just be over already so she could go back to her life again. Rolling to a stop at the end of the school parking lot she wasn't paying close enough attention to the road, while changing the radio station, and almost drove right into a dirty, green jeep pulling up next to her. The boy behind the wheel looked furious and wouldn't drop eye contact with Sophia, like he was mad but also trying to look at her better. Shocked and embarrassed, she shied away behind her steering wheel and flew out of there.

CHAPTER FOUR

Her dad's house was easy to find, right on a busy main road with minimal parking space. The house was small and cramped and her room was no better. It was a hideous baby blue with sun stained, off white drapes hanging from the dirty windows that looked out to another small, old house. There was a twin sized bed in one corner and across from it sat a lumpy old couch, buried under boxes and bags. She soon noticed that the closet would hardly be able to hold half of her clothes in it and this was a major problem. She had enough clothing, thanks to her grandfathers' unlimited supply of credit card usage, to dress the whole town.

Dropping her school bag and books on the only available space in her floor she fell back onto the bare mattress and sent Lucy a text:

1 day down. 364 days to go. I miss you!):

"Now what?" Sophia thought out loud as she looked around at her disaster of a room. She needed to cover up the gross blue walls and fast. She thought she'd start with a mirror. As she put it up on a couple tacks she noticed the status of her unruly hair. The humidity had made it so frizzy it grew in volume three times its normal size. Her face looked even more pale than usual and her dark green eyes looked sad and miserable in this empty room. She was unique with her vivid red hair and exceptional emerald green eyes. Her mother always told her she was special because of it, but she loathed standing out so much. Pushing her heavy rimmed, black glasses up on her nose better, and throwing her hair up in a thick, messy bun, she got to work with the rest of her room.

Two hours and three boxes of clothes and trinkets later and she was ready to pass out on her still unmade, tiny mattress. She had only been able to put some clothes in the closet and some picture frames of her and Lucy on the window sills and bedside table. But after her stressful day of school on top of everything else, she decided to give up. So, pulling a quilt over her exhausted body, she called it a day and fell asleep.

Her dreams were an interwoven kaleidoscope of memories and fantasy. People's faces she didn't know and long hallways that never ended. She kept running and running, trying to find an exit from the relentless onslaught of fluorescent light and the harsh stare of strangers. Finally, at what seemed like the end of the hallway, there was a boy. His back was toward her, but as she approached he turned around, slowly. It was the boy from the green jeep, with his piercing dark eyes driving straight into her soul. With a blank face, he reached out his hand to her, but before she could react, he swished away in a puff of black smoke and she awoke with a start, suddenly staring at a baby blue wall in a stuffy little room.

CHAPTER FIVE

Charlie could not get the girl with red hair out of his head. He hadn't even talked to her but somehow, he believed deep down he knew her. He kept seeing fleeting images of himself as a young boy with a girl that had such unbelievable features. He saw himself playing in the woods with her in a little pink dress as he slayed the numerous bush creatures that stole her away from him. In all these flashes of memories not once did she turn her face to him completely, it was like trying to look through a pair of glasses that were smudged with finger prints. He could see her, but he couldn't. All these random memories he so easily forgot were flashing in his mind, but he couldn't quite put a name or a time to that strange flicker of a girl. As he continued the day in school the recollections finally subsided and he focused more on what he was doing. Yet as soon as he saw her again they all came back just as strong. At lunch he noticed that she sat with his good friends' girlfriend Claire, but he couldn't get himself to go over and talk to her. She was beautiful, but not like the typical high school cheerleader girl stereotype. She was different then any girl he'd ever seen and she acted like nothing in the world could ever faze her, he couldn't understand her. And that bothered him.

CHAPTER SIX

Months into the school year later and Charlie was making it down to the locker room just in time for his big football game. He had taken an extra shift at work right after school to cover someone who called out sick, but there was no way he would miss his game. They were playing against the second greatest team in the high school football league and he couldn't wait to get out on the field and use his well-trained muscles to tackle and run and play his favorite sport. His curiosity about Sophia had simmered enough that he wasn't constantly dreaming about her at nights and he was all about the new football season now. All he wanted was to take his team to the top and this was his year to prove to the scouts that he was good enough for any college football team out there.

As he jogged out to the bench a flash of color caught his eye in the crowd above him, stopping him in his tracks. That same red hair that always caught his eye, was sitting in the first row of bleachers looking straight at him.

CHAPTER SEVEN

Sophia couldn't stop staring at him. Ever since she started going to school here she noticed him watching her, and she could never understand why. He by no means tried talking to her; he never even came close enough to her so she could talk to him. It was as if he was trying to avoid her even though they didn't know each other. The dream she had of him haunted her still and every so often he would show up in her waking sleep and taunt her. He never spoke to her, he would just look her straight in the eyes. It was becoming unbearable. She had enough of it though. Today after the game she planned on confronting him. If anything, she needed to prove that he was just a rude jock that would never want to talk to her. Then it would be easier to forget about him and move on with her life. Lucy suggested the idea of confronting him and asking why he avoided her so aggressively. If only her nerves would allow it. *Maybe another day...* she procrastinated. She thought that maybe she was just crazy and he hadn't been staring at her after all and if she confronted him about it he'd think she was crazy.

"There he is again, staring at you." Claire said to Sophia and she turned the other way to her boyfriend Joey,

"Babe, what's his deal. He has like some huge crush on my girl or what?"

"I don't think so. He never talks about her." Joey said after he took a moment to think about it.

“That’s so annoying.” Claire muttered while applying a fresh coat of cherry flavored, pink lip gloss, and fixed her eye make-up with a small pink compact mirror she always kept in her pink knock off Prada bag. It had only taken Sophia a few days to figure out that Claire’s favorite color was quite obviously pink. She hadn’t seen Claire a single day without some amount of pink on her and Sophia wondered if she even knew about the rest of the colors in this world.

After Charlie’s team won the intense game and the bleachers were clear of people and left with empty soda bottles and candy wrappers, Sophia and Claire left Joey and went to the parking lot with a group of other people they had been sitting with. Everyone was so happy about the win, but Sophia could not care any less. She wasn’t really into the whole sports thing and had only come because Claire begged her to.

“You need some social interaction outside of school girl! People are gonna start thinking you’re some freak that never leaves her room.” Claire had joked. But the thought of being known as the school ‘freak’ was enough to make Sophia go. It was bad enough her red hair made her stick out as much as it did.

As a kid she did gymnastics just because her mom thought it was good for her, but almost every little girl did gymnastics growing up so it was nothing special. Just another way parents make sure their kids lose some energy before having to deal with it themselves. She wouldn’t have minded it so much if it was just for fun, but all the other girls were there to train for medals in hopes to someday make their parents dreams of being in the Olympics’ come true. That was the extent of Sophia’s athletic career. After that she was happy just to sit at home and play or read. She never grew up watching sports either. The idea of watching people run back and forth on a huge field was less than appealing to her. She would rather do something more creative and useful. She enjoyed spending time with Claire and Joey, though, so she didn't completely hate watching the football game at school.

As the girls started walking towards Sophia's car, Joey ran up next to Claire and started telling her all about some party that was going on that night to celebrate the big win. Sophia wasn't paying much attention to what she was doing, while trying to hear him better, when her car keys slipped out of her fingers. Just before they dropped to the damp pavement someone scooped them out of the air and held them dangling in front of her face.

"Good reflex huh?" Charlie said with a small, mischievous grin. His hair was still damp under his cap from the shower and he smelled strongly of his shampoo and cologne.

"Umm, sure." Sophia said precariously as she snatched her keys, unlocked her car, and threw her bag in the back seat. She couldn't believe for a second that he was, finally, really talking to her. And then she couldn't believe she was still able to stand. Her heart was starting to flutter fretfully and eagerly as she turned back around to face him. As she leaned her back against the car, and coolly crossed her arms over her chest so she didn't look so timid, she locked eyes with Charlie. She attempted a strong, confident look, but ended up just looking like a little kid that didn't get her way. Charlie didn't seem to notice, or care.

"You going to the party tonight?" he said. She noticed he would not lose eye contact; Just kept staring right at her, barely even blinking. It was making her extremely uncomfortable and for a second she considered running away from him so as to not make a fool of herself trying to sound like she wasn't as tense as she really was.

"I don't know, I'll be with Claire so really it's up to her." Looking to her left she saw that Claire and Joey were leaned up against the back of her car, kissing as shamelessly as if they didn't realize they were in the middle of a crowded parking lot.

"I'll take that as a yes," Charlie said slowly with a smirk, clearly trying to hold back laughter. "See you tonight!"

And with that he was gone. Sophia didn't even have time to say anything back to him. *Why did he even care?* She thought as she watched Claire push herself away from Joey playfully and run around to the passenger side of Sophia's car.

CHAPTER EIGHT

They were on their way to Sophia's first high school party ever. There were always parties in her old school but they were busted almost every single time so Sophia stayed away from them. She'd never even had alcohol to drink before so she was a little anxious about being thrown into the party scene for the first time tonight. She also had a good feeling that this wasn't Claire's first time so she was desperately hoping to not get ditched.

"It's this house up on the right I think. So you gonna talk to Charlie tonight?" Claire questioned.

"I don't know. Why not I guess?" Sophia replied. She felt as if she was giving in to some huge ordeal when it was really no big deal at all. It's just some dumb senior boy who probably wants to hook up with her for the night. She'll hear out his pitch of how he 'can't live without her and she's oh-so-beautiful' and then she'll shut him down, hopefully ending his weird staring contests in the hallways between classes, and at lunch, and in the parking lots...

Irritatingly the only available space to park for this party was a block away from the house. But as Sophia and Claire started walking down the dimly lit road they could already hear the music. Once the door was open, they could barely get through the mob of people playing drinking games and dancing and throwing a football above everyone's heads. A group of kids in one corner were covered in a cloud of cigar smoke playing card games Sophia had never heard of and on the couch was a couple that were obviously already drunk as they kissed without even once coming up for air. Some random guy handed the girls drinks, which splashed up over the rim and down her hand, and Sophia had to hold her breath just to take a small sip.

"What is this, poison?" she said, coughing instantly after opening her mouth, and in return Claire just gave her an admiring glance and laughed a little, as if Sophia were a child asking what a cloud was.

"Drink up girl, we gotta get you to stop shaking somehow. You're starting to me make nervous geez..." Claire said as she tipped her cup back and downed half of the appalling liquids inside. Sophia knew that she was in for a long night already.

After a few drinks and following Claire around for a couple hours and talking to some girls she had a few classes with Sophia needed some fresh air and found a back door leading out to a surprisingly quiet, secluded inground pool. Rolling her jeans up to her knees and putting down her fourth strong drink of the night she dipped her feet into the cool water and lay back against the rough cement that surrounded the heavily chlorinated pool. Just as she finally got the world to stop spinning she heard foot steps followed by an all too familiar voice that she didn't want to hear at that moment.

"Am I interrupting anything?" Charlie said as he walked around the pool to her side. '*Why do you have to be so hot?!*' Sophia thought as her eyes slowly focused in on his face.

"You're only interrupting my death, have you had one of these drinks? The sky won't stop moving." She felt like her eyes weighed twenty pounds each as they strained to meet Charlie's.

"How many of these have you had?" he said taking a sip as if it were water to him. *What was with these people up here?* She thought, amazed at how easy it was for everyone to drink whatever kept going around when she could barely stand the smell.

"I think that's my fourth, maybe my fifth, I don't know anymore. What do you want?" she'd had enough of being the shy new girl around here, and the drinks helped a bit with her forceful attitude.

"I just wanted to see how you're doing. Didn't want you to fall in the pool and drown." He said jokingly.

"Drowning doesn't sound so bad right now." Sophia said as she attempted to lift herself up and instantly had to lie back down. Not only was the world spinning, but now her stomach was joining it.

"I hope you don't take this the wrong way, but do I know you from somewhere? I feel like I do and I can't stop thinking about it."

"How would I know? You probably don't even know my name." she said looking up into his stunning eyes. Thinking more about it he did look like someone she'd seen before, but she couldn't tell how or where. She also thought that he probably did know her name by now but was just humoring her at this point.

"Well are you going to tell me, or do I have to ask your blonde friend, who is currently eating the face off Joey in some ones room upstairs?" Charlie said back as he laughed a little and sat down with his legs crossed in front of him.

"Sophia." She said while reaching her hand out to shake his, but after she said it he looked shocked and didn't take her unsteady hand, dangling out in front of her. As if someone just slapped him across the face, he was frozen in the expression of shock. He had known her name before now, but once she said it and he was so close to her he suddenly realized what he had been missing all along.

"Sophia? Did you used to live here a long time ago?" he asked her with hesitance. It was like he didn't want to know, but had to.

"Like ten years ago, why? How'd you know that?" she sat up now ignoring the constant feeling of intense nausea and faced him. He grabbed her hand and moved closer to her.

"I knew it! Sophia it's me, Charlie. How can you not recognize me? I know it's been a while and last time you saw me we were so young, but I know you remember me. You have to." Just as the words came out of his mouth it clicked. It was her Charlie. The little boy she loved and played with every single day. The little boy she told everything to, and played princess and prince in the woods behind their houses. Her breath caught in her throat as it all registered. And even in her drunken state she knew this was really happening. With all the years that had gone by and all the changes in him she never even had the slightest memory of Charlie when she looked at him. She was still skeptical of this new discovery, but at the moment she didn't seem to care so much.

"Charlie! That's why you kept staring at me? Oh my gosh, this isn't real." She couldn't help herself and she jumped up on him and hugged him without even thinking, knocking her drink over in the process. She didn't even care; she couldn't believe it was really him. She held him in the embrace as the pool water on her legs splashed and the drink tipped over and spilt around them, soaking their pants. She forgot all about him over the years and he had grown up so much she couldn't even tell. Of course her hair is a dead give away, no one has hair this red besides a little mermaid named Ariel. He hugged her right back just as hard.

"I'm not letting you go this time." He said and he meant it. He knew they were just kids last time he saw her but somehow she still meant everything to him. She was like the mystery he had never been able to solve all those years after she had gone. She was the best part of his childhood and every memory he had of growing up included her. They talked for what seemed like forever about the past ten years. How she grew up in an all girls private school, and how her parents never talk anymore because her dad was caught cheating when she was a little girl.

"My mom said that we were just going on vacation at my papas' house and my dad was too busy to go. When we never went back she said it was because they didn't like each other anymore. It wasn't until I was thirteen that she told me the truth." Sophia just barely remembered that night, all those years ago. She remembered how sad and defeated her dad looked as her and her mom drove away; she just sat quietly in the back seat holding her doll tightly to her chest, wishing it was all just a bad dream..

Just then her phone vibrated with a new text. She could barely keep her eyes focused on the tiny, bright screen and struggled to read the message from Claire:

Where are you?! Cops were tipped, lets go! xoClaire

"I have to go. I hope I see you again!" She said searching his eyes for more answers about what just happened. She was still a little shocked from it all and still very drunk.

"Don't worry, you will." And he helped her up and watched her waveringly walk away. She gave him one last glance over her shoulder as she stumbled through the back door and into the loud music and chaos.

CHAPTER NINE

She met Claire in the front yard and they walked as fast as any two drunken girls in flip flops could manage.

"Who's going to drive my car?" Sophia questioned as they came up to her car.

"No one, you're parked far enough away from the house, lets just get out of here! Ill have my mom pick us up." And with that they rounded the block, which felt like ten miles away and sat messily on the sidewalk, waiting for their ride. Sophia was so dizzy between the thought of seeing Charlie again and the amounts of alcohol sloshing around inside her from walking. The world around her started to spin again but this time she couldn't contain the movement and she leaned out to the side and threw up.

The rest of the night was a haze to her as she barely noticed herself getting in a car and someone soon after pushing her roughly into Claire's bed.

The next morning was not something she could so easily have forgotten though.

Sophia woke up in an unfamiliar room, with the sun streaming directly on her face. Her head was in such immense pain she almost thought she had been hit by a car last night and was now in a hospital regaining consciousness from a five day coma. The dryness of her throat made her groan as she rolled over out of the painfully bright sun and understood that this is what it felt like to be hung over. It was at that moment that an all too happy Claire sat next to her on the plush pink bed spread with three Advil in one hand and a bottle of ginger ale in the other.

"So how do you feel besides like crap?" she said as Sophia downed all three pills at once and looked up at her as if she was insane.

"How are you so lively? Did you even drink last night?" Sophia said in a hoarse voice she didn't recognize that made her throat sore.

"Not as much as you did apparently!" she said and then continued on to say that Joey was on his way, it was one in the afternoon, and she had to go home.

So Claire dropped her off at her car and Sophia drove back to her house, remembering that she hadn't even told her dad she wasn't going to be coming home last night. He was probably furious with her and she wanted so badly to not have to deal with him with the amount of pain she was suffering from in her head and stomach. She had no way of texting him because her phone died at some point last night. The drive home was nice enough though, as the wind blew her tangled, red hair around her face and she got lost in thoughts of Charlie and the crazy idea that they actually found each other again.

She thought back to that day when she was so little, and her life changed so abruptly. It started on one sunny Sunday morning; Sophia woke up around seven just like always, expecting the smell of breakfast to be floating around her doll filled room, but something wasn't right. She couldn't even smell her parent's strong, bitter coffee. As she flung the purple, flowery comforter off herself and slide her tiny feet into the fluffy pink, kitten slippers at the side of her bed, she skipped out her door and started down the stairs. Stopping at the bottom, she peeked her head around the wall to the kitchen and saw her parents sitting at the table, staring at each other in a way that scared Sophia a little.

Neither of them was saying a word, but her mom didn't look very amused at whatever her father had just told her. Sophia had never seen either of them acting the way they were and she wasn't sure what to think of it, but the second she walked fully into the kitchen they both suddenly put on big smiles and greeted her with a kiss on the head and offered her a pop-tart. Not exactly what she expected. As she sat down at the table to eat her dry blueberry pop-tart her parents bustled about the house avoiding each other at all costs. But she thought nothing more of it at the time.

Their strange behaviors began to happen more often and more presently as the week continued until finally, they broke into a huge fight one late afternoon; the fight that changed everything. Sophia was told to go her room and pack her favorite outfits and dolls in a tiny suitcase her mom roughly handed her. An hour later her mom came through the door with tears streaming down her face just as Sophia was buttoning on her dolly's pink shirt.

"Time to go." She said to Sophia and walked back out of her room.

"Where are we going daddy?" Sophia said as she used all her strength to bring her stuff down the wooden staircase.

"Just be a good girl baby, I love you so much. Don't ever forget that..." he went to give her a hug as a tear rolled down his cheek, but he was too slow and her mom violently grabbed Sophia's arm and walked out the door.

The last thing Sophia could remember was clutching her favorite baby doll and looking back towards her house, watching her parents yelling at each other like she'd never seen before, not knowing that she wouldn't return for years.

CHAPTER TEN

Pulling into her driveway she noticed her dad was staring out the living room window, holding back the drapes to get a better view. She was certain he was beyond mad at her so she put on the most apologetic face she could muster and walked up to the front door. Barely two steps in the house and she knew she was in for it.

"Have fun last night?" her dad said curtly with an 'I'm not amused' face on. The kind of face that teenagers always know as the face parents put on right before sentencing them to a terrible punishment of which they will attempt to fight and will always lose.

"Would it help my case if I said I'm really, really sorry and it'll never happen again?" she said trying to put on the cutest, most innocent face she could muster.

"Not so much. You're grounded." He said firmly, ending the discussion completely. And with that she headed upstairs to sleep off the horrid pain in her head that now seemed so much worse.

CHAPTER ELEVEN

The weekend was far too long for Charlie to handle. He just wanted to see her again. He wanted to know every single thing about her. Watching her walk away from him at that party was torture. He knew she was a different person now, but they were so close all those years ago. That had to mean something.

He had gotten her cell phone number from Claire the day after, but she wasn't responding to any of his texts. Charlie was not as concerned about that though because he knew that Claire wasn't getting ahold of her either. Assuming she must have been grounded from staying out all that night he let it roll off his shoulders and focused on training. He felt himself relax and calm as he lifted weights and jogged on the treadmill. She would be in school, and then he could talk to her again. He was so distracted by the fact that he hardly paid attention to his parents around the house, which they thought was unusual behavior for him. He was usually always watching sports with his dad or helping his mom with the house work. He was too distracted by this new feeling gripping his chest that he could do nothing but pour himself into his work and exercise.

Finally, Monday came around and Charlie was again pulling his creaky jeep into the school parking lot. His usual lack of amusement he felt coming to school was now replaced with an excitement he usually only had for football. It was a strange thing to him to feel this way about a girl, but he knew she was not just any girl. He was amazed to find himself catching sight of her in the parking lot, as she was removing her bag from the back seat. Charlie half walked half ran over to her and stopped just at the trunk of her very nice, new car.

“Hello again.” Charlie said as she noticed his presence. Pushing back a lock of her typically lively hair, she smiled up at him.

“Hello. I’m surprised you’re here right now, after the mess I made of myself at the party.” Sophia said, her face turning a crimson red. Charlie thought it was cute the way she became so shy.

“I meant it when I told you I would never let you go again.” He said boldly. Sophia was shocked that he would say such a thing without having been drunk like the previous time they were so blunt together. She figured that night was just liquid courage. It gave Sophia a burst of her own confidence.

“Well I’m here now, so tell me, what you are going to do to make sure I’m never let go.” Sophia surprised herself with her mindless comment, this behavior was so unlike her own she was worried to make a fool of herself by trying too hard. To her amusement Charlie had more confidence than she had first judged. He laughed, the sound was smooth and captivating to Sophia; he grabbed her hand and gave a wink. Then continued to walk towards school, Sophia in tow.

This was a big deal. For Charlie to be walking into a crowd of students with a girl in his hand was absurd to say the least. It would signify the first time he had ever shown a liking to something or someone more than football or himself. Every girl who ever made a pass at him would be gritting their teeth flat to the gum if they were to see. How dare the new girl catch the eye of the unapproachable Charlie? It made Sophia nervous as though it were her first day in the new school all over again.

"Charlie, what are you doing! Are you sure about this…" she said, but even as she was saying it Charlie tightened his grip and pulled her closer to his side.
"If it's ok with you, I think I'm more than positive about this." Sophia was not about to turn that down, but she was confused. What did this mean?

The pair entered school and just as one would imagine they were instant eye magnets. No one that saw them could understand what was happening before their eyes. It was impossible that the two would ever become a couple, but here they were. Though the entirety of the school was ignorant of Sophia and Charlie's fleeting history together, which made it all the more confusing for them and evermore exciting for Sophia and Charlie.

Having had no classes together they split up and went on through the day as they normally would have, only now it seemed that Sophia had some type of ranking among the other students. They regarded her a bit more highly, some even attempting to make small talk with her.
"So are you guys like, a thing now?" Claire asked Sophia the second she sat down in their first class together.
"No, I mean, I don't think so. He just wanted to hold my hand I guess. We don't even really know each other." She replied.
"Just wanted to hold your hand. Right." Claire did not believe a word of it. She looked hurt to be left out of such an important loop, but after a few minutes she moved on and was complaining about her cuticles and how Joey didn't send her a 'good morning text'.

They day drew on like it never had before. Sophia was anxious to see Charlie again if only to solidify whatever it was that happened that morning. Taking her time to get back to her car she was dragging her feet, but to her disbelief she noticed him out in the parking lot, leaning up against her car as if he owned it.

"Is he my boyfriend.?" Sophia thought out loud as she made her way across the final stretch of pavement between them.

"Hello beautiful." Charlie said as she came to a stop in front of him.

"What is happening Charlie, really." She couldn't take the anxiety anymore, she had to know.

"I'm not sure what you mean, all I said was that you're beautiful." He said with a grin.

"But, why? What are... we?" Sophia finally asked the question that had been running around in her head all day. Her heart was beating faster, and she noticed her hands became cold and clammy. They had one solid conversation together, it wasn't like they were even really friends yet. Why would she even consider he wanted to be her boyfriend already. This was all so weird to Sophia, but she could not stop hoping it was going to happen. She was crazy attracted to him and they got along well and for some insane reason he actually liked her. She held her breath as he began to reply.

"Well, I was thinking that maybe, and I know this is crazy, but maybe you could be my girlfriend?" It was the first time Sophia had ever seen Charlie look afraid, a fact that completely snapped her out of her own anxiety and filled her stomach with a fluttering sensation.

"Yes." She said with a solid and confident boldness. She was so sure of this that she surprised herself with the certainty.

"So, do you want to hang out, maybe right now?" Charlie said. His shyness was replaced with a sense of pride and excitement. He casually reached for her hand, and rubbed his thumb across her soft skin.

"Okay." She said. She felt like she was entering a world totally unknown to her. She had never had a boyfriend before. She had never shared her life with anyone besides Lucy, and that was hardly the same. A guy liked her! He wasn't afraid of her looks or her awkwardness. She felt her stomach turn in the most amazing way and her head was in the clouds and she could finally understand what Claire was always going on about when she talked about Joey.

CHAPTER TWELVE

They decided to leave Sophia's car at school and they both hopped into Charlie's green jeep. The ride to his house wasn't long, but it felt like it lasted forever. Sophia was still in a state of happiness and shock since leaving the parking lot. And Charlie seemed just as excited as she was. He held her hand in her lap in between changing the gears and they rode to his house in silent contentment. He drove the same route he always did, but now it felt different. It was his first time driving Sophia to his house, or so he thought at first, until he remembered that she used to live just next door.

"I wonder if I will remember what my house looked like, it's been so long..." Sophia said quietly as they came up to the neighborhood. Her dad didn't live in her childhood house for very long after her and her mother left him. It was too big and too expensive for a single person to live in alone. He sold it within the first year they were gone and moved to the other side of town into a small split level. It was old and unkempt, but it was his place of healing after the divorce. They ended their marriage because he cheated on Sophia's mother, but he never entered a relationship with the woman he cheated with. It was a onetime mistake and he regretted every second of it.

"Not much has changed except that they cleared out some trees and put up a big fence. The fence would have never worked for our bottle notes…" Charlie said. He looked sideways at her to see if she would remember and after a moment she smiled to herself. He knew she remembered. As kids they used to sneak over to each other's houses and hide little notes trapped inside empty plastic water bottles. It was their secret way of communicating when they weren't able to hang out.

"It will still feel weird being back here. What will your parents think? They will not believe this." Sophia laughed, a tight nervous laugh that gave away all her hidden anxiety. She was more nervous to see his parents again than to be spending time alone with him.

He pulled his jeep into its spot in the garage and put it in park. Neither of them moved.

"So, I haven't told them about you yet. I haven't really talked to anyone about you, not even Joey…" he said.

"Yes, I've heard. Why is that? Are you embarrassed?" she asked him. The thought suddenly dawning on her.

"Obviously not. There's nothing I want more than you." His unexpected nerve surprised both of them. He spoke without thinking and there was no retracting his words now.

"I don't understand how you can say that, you don't even know me anymore, not really." Sophia said, but she said it with a kindness that let him know she wasn't mad about his statement. She took ahold of his hand and smiled.

"Ah, reason number one, that amazing smile. I could stare at that smile all day." He said.

"Well, I think we've been there and done that before." Laughed Sophia, "Okay let's do this before I freak out."

As she stepped out of his jeep she noticed his side of the garage was not just used for his car, but also had his weights, a roughed-up couch, and a small fridge in one corner. A table with unfamiliar tools and smears of black, shiny grease covered the top, while underneath were cardboard boxes. Each box had words scribbled across the side, but due to time and dust they were barely legible. The other side, where his parents parked their cars was spotless and swept clean. With organized shelves, clearly labeled, and a couple of sparkling new bikes hanging up on the wall.

"Do you hang out in here Charlie?" Sophia asked him. She was suddenly curious about everything he did with his life. Where did he love to hang out, what were his chores, where did he sleep… *'do not think about that! Not going to go there…'* she had to distract herself from her own thoughts and picked up a greasy tool.

"Yeah, I love my parents, but sometimes they are just too sunshine and rainbows for me… you'll see. Uh, you're probably going to want to wash your hands now." Charlie grabbed her hand, which was still clutching the wrench she had picked up, and turned her palm to face her. Where the tool had touched her hand was now a large black smear. Sophia laughed nervously and looked up at him.

"Oh my gosh I am so sorry! What do I do?" her face turned red as she looked around for something to wipe her hand on.

"It's okay, come with me." He wrapped his arm around her waist and turned her toward the door leading inside. This was the closest they had been since she hugged him by the pool. Her face turned a shade darker as he kept his hand on the bottom of her back and walked into the house. She silently begged that his parents were busy doing something before her hand was cleaned, but she wasn't that lucky. Just on the other side of the door was both his mother and father, standing there with bright eyes and wide smiles.

"Hello there! How are you? You are just a peach, what is your name dear?" his mother came right over and held her hand out for Sophia to shake.

"Oh, umm, well my hand is… I'm Sophia. I think we've met before, you know, like forever ago…" she gave a short, nervous laugh and looked up at his mother's face just as it registered to her who Sophia was. Sophia was so embarrassed at her rambling and the fact that her first impression was with greasy hands, had it not been for Charlie holding her waist she would have passed out.

His mother silently looked up at Charlie and then back at Sophia with wide eyes before she said another word.

"Well, I can't say that I ever thought I would see you again, but I am certainly not mad about it! I am so happy to see you again, you must be the reason my Charlie has been in such a strange and wonderful mood these past few days!" Her smile was happy and inviting. It instantly settled Sophia's anxieties and she smiled back at her. Never in a million years did Sophia think she would be in this situation. They exchanged a few quick pleasantries before excusing themselves to wash up.

Once Sophia was cleaned up, Charlie brought her to his room. It was a total mess. Clothes all over the floor, footballs of varying deflation were shoved under his bed, and the sheets on his mattress were hanging off the bed.

"I'm sorry it's such a mess, I really didn't plan on having you over today, but I'm so happy you are here." Charlie took her hand again and they settled on a small couch next to his bed. There they sat and they talked, for hours. He occasionally brushed his hand across her leg or played with her hand, but he did not make any attempt to push things further. Sophia was enjoying just being with him. She kept expecting it to feel like old times, but it wasn't like old times. They were both almost eighteen now, they were matured and had different feelings for each other than they did ten years ago. This was new to both Charlie and Sophia. Instead of making forts for stuffed animals, they were talking about plans for the future, their favorite food, and what music they liked to listen to. Charlie sat with his legs stretched out in front of him and an arm across the back of the couch and Sophia had her legs crisscrossed under her while facing him. They sat like that for what felt like ages. Neither of them wanted to move

When the darkness of night was closing in around them Sophia decided she should go home, reluctant though she was at leaving him. They had spent their entire evening talking and laughing and Sophia never wanted it to end. With each passing hour she felt more and more for him. They shared a connection that no one could duplicate. A connection made from their past history and also the immense chemical attraction they shared. They seemed to be, quite literally, perfect for each other. Where one failed the other was strongest. Where one was unsure the other was confident. They balanced each other. They were the definition of opposites attracting one another.

Charlie drove Sophia back to the, now empty, school parking lot. The dim parking lot lights up above were flickering and swarmed with moths. Charlie gathered Sophia's hands in his and stared into her green eyes.

"Goodnight." He whispered and he gently kissed where her ear met her cheek. He held his kiss for just a moment before pulling away, smiling at her brightly, and turned to leave.

Sophia stood there, basking in the lingering feel of his lips against her cheek, and watched as he drove away. His elbow hung out the open window and the breeze brushed his hair out of his face as he left her sight, still smiling.

Lucy, you will never believe this. Call me! Now!! □

She drove home replaying their time together. She walked through her house in a daze and landed on her bed. Lucy did not text her back that night, but Sophia didn't mind. She was too happy to care about anything. She drifted off to sleep with thoughts of Charlie and fell into a deep and dreamless state of comfort she had never known before. She was accepted at the highest level and by someone who she truly cared about. She wanted to scream it at the top of her lungs and hide him away from everyone all at once.

CHAPTER THIRTEEN

Charlie couldn't focus on anything besides Sophia his entire ride home. She was everything he never knew he wanted. She was perfect in every way. His good mood lasted all the way to his garage and to the door and no further.

The door inside the garage was busted open, the handle dangling to the side. He had left the garage door open when he left to bring Sophia home, but he never would have thought someone would break in. Looking around cautiously he noticed both his parent's cars were still home. He immediately become aware of a pounding in his ears and the blood rushed out of his head with the most disturbing speed.

Slowly pushing forward the door, he stepped in and took in the scene that was, only thirty minutes ago, his happy and peaceful home. The tables were thrown across the floor, plates and bowls smashed to pieces on every surface, drawers were pulled out of their spots in the kitchen, and the couches were slashed to shreds. He looked frantically in every direction, but there was no one around. He heard nothing and he saw nothing and he had no idea what to do. Frozen in the midst of the chaos he was struck dumb and was unable to make a coherent thought. Not until his eyes fell upon a shattered picture frame did he think about his parents. They were still home when this happened.

Charlie ran upstairs after quickly sweeping through the downstairs rooms. He was certain whoever did this was long gone and he was desperately looking for his parents. The upstairs was just as trashed as everywhere else. All electronics and valuable trinkets were gone, blank empty space was all that remained on the walls and counters where they once lived. He reached the double doorway to his parent's room and saw them both lying still on the floor.

"No! Mom, Dad! Mom!" he flung himself on the floor and rolled his mother onto her back. She was still breathing, but her neck was purple and red and in some spots Charlie could make out the shape of a finger. She must have been strangled. He held his mother tight and looked over to his dad. His throat caught and his breathing stopped in his chest and he knew, without even touching his father he knew, he was dead.

His face had been punched so hard and so many times he was unrecognizable, and his neck hung at an unnatural angle. His body was limp and motionless and twisting in all directions. Charlie was so horrified at what he saw he forgot that his mother was still alive and breathing.

"Mom, it's okay. I'm here, its Charlie. It's okay mom, it's okay…" tears streamed down his cheeks as he clutched her to his chest. Her breath was soft and staggered. He knew he had to call the police and ambulance, but his limbs were frozen in place. He sat there and cried over his mother. Cried like he had never cried before and held her.

After a few minutes he slowly, gently placed his mother on the floor and called the police with his cell phone. All the house phones were taken. He told the operator what happened and that his mother needed emergency medical attention, he gave them all the necessary information, and he hung up.

Charlie leaned against the wall and heaved. He threw up across the bedroom floor, across his mom's favorite imported rug, and his dad's loafers, and it didn't matter. Why would it matter now? What was his life now? What was he going to do? His father lay dead and bloodied, just mere hours after talking to him. He was gone, just like that.

Charlie always imagined that when his parents time had come they would be old and grey and holding their grandbabies close, and surrounded by family. He never once imagined that they would be home, feeling safe, and not thinking twice when the door in the kitchen that lead to the garage was kicked open it would be the last thing they saw. His parents were brutalized in their own home. His sense of security had all but vanished faster than the blink of an eye.

While Charlie sat next to his vomit, crying and trembling with fear and grief, he heard a hard knock and the emergency responder's voices echoing up the stairs.

He remembered calling them into the bedroom and the bright lights bouncing around the room from their flashlights and questions and blankets being wrapped around him. A woman's voice trying to soothe him. He didn't hear words, only muted sounds, like he was holding a phone away from his ear while someone yelled on the other line. His head was in a fog, like he was swimming, but could never reach the air in time to breathe. Yet, he never suffocated.

She took his cell phone and called the first person on his calling list that wasn't his parents.

With the help of another EMT he was moved to the living room, and placed upon the shredded couch cushions while the rest of them moved his parents to the ambulances outside. Soon after, an officer came over to him and asked him more questions. Who did this? Do you have any reason to suspect your parents had enemies? What is missing?

"I don't know…" is all he could say in response. His tears, a hot steady stream, swept down his cheeks and puddled on the grey, wool blanket he had wrapped around his body. More officers were arriving, and more red and blue lights began to shine off of every wall and ceiling in the house. Charlie felt like he was in a madhouse, a haunted house. With ghosts and lights and dark unknown spaces. This wasn't his home anymore. This would never be his home again.

An hour must have passed before a familiar face came into focus. Charlie was beginning to breathe more regularly, though everything was still in a state of shock. Joey and Claire came running up to him through the mass of detectives and police.

"Charlie! Dude, what the hell happened? What happened to your house? Where are your parents? Charlie, what happened?" Joey was panicked and Claire was starting to cry looking around at the scene of chaos. Charlie stood up from his spot on the ruined couch.

"I don't know… I came home and I found, this. My parents, my dad, he's…" it was enough to bring Charlie to tears again.

"Charlie, no… he can't be." Joey grabbed him by the shoulder and shook his body, "he can't be, okay, he'll be fine. All these people here, he'll be fine."

"He's dead Joey. And my mom probably is too. They're both just, gone." Charlie slumped down on the floor, his body giving out and cried. Joey and Claire knelt and held him and they stayed there until the house cleared out and they were told to leave.

Charlie spent that night at Joey's house, though he didn't sleep. He lay there and came to terms with what had happened. His father was dead, that he was sure. His mother was in the hospital under critical condition and he wasn't allowed to see her until further notice. Her throat was wrung so hard they had to reconstruct her trachea and insert a breathing tube. Her food would now be delivered through a hole in her stomach, as far as Charlie had understood the ER doctor. She would never be the same again. She can't talk and she can't breathe and she can't eat. She was a vegetable. How could she even mourn the loss of her husband? She was trapped in a useless body with little to no chance of recovery.

Charlie tossed and turned and cried and shook and had cold sweats the rest of the night. He couldn't accept or understand what had happened.

CHAPTER FOURTEEN

Three days passed before Sophia heard from Charlie. After Claire told her what happened Sophia wanted nothing more than to run to Charlie and hold him and comfort him, but Claire said he was far from receptive. Sophia cried and hugged Claire and wished he could have any form of relief from his suffering. When her father found out he dropped everything and went straight to the hospital. Sophia forgot how close of friends their parents had been. They grew up together almost as similarly as Charlie and Sophia did. His loss was nearly equal to what Charlie must be feeling.

I'm here for you... text me when you're ready. XO

Sophia had to reach out to him, she couldn't bear the thought of him suffering through this.

Sophia, Claire, and Joey all returned to school that Monday feeling disconnected to the rest of the world. Sophia felt almost ashamed to even be in school and acting like nothing happened, she felt like she was betraying Charlie by going on with her life, but she didn't know what else to do. No one tells you how to react to a situation like this. No one tells you how hard it is. They weren't even her parents and she was feeling such a deep loss.

She hadn't been expecting Charlie to answer her, not so soon anyway, when she got a text during fourth period that day:

I need to see you. I'll be at your car after school.

Her breath caught in her chest and a sudden wave of anxiety flushed over her. She still had two periods left before school was out, still two more hours before she could see him.

She fidgeted and tapped her feet and flipped through her books the entire rest of her day until finally the last bell rang and she flung herself out of her chair and ran down the hall.

As she made her way through the maze of cars she bounced on the tips of her toes to get a better view to where she had parked. She could just barely make out the top of his head, his favorite baseball cap pulled tightly over his shaggy brown hair. His usually tan skin was now a shade paler and his shoulders slumped inward where they once were strong and confident. He was a different person than the last time she saw him and it frightened her.

Sophia brushed aside her fears as she rounded the back of a pick-up, dropped her bag to the pavement and wrapped her arms around Charlies neck. It was a moment before he returned her embrace, but when he did he held her in place for what felt like ten minutes. Sophia looked up into his eyes and noticed they were rimmed in dark red and he had bags under his eyes that he never had before. He looked broken completely. His appearance caused a tear to fall, silently, from Sophia's eye and she hugged him tighter.

"I'm so sorry Charlie, I'm so sorry. What can I do? Are you okay? I'm here for you, I promise I'll do whatever it takes to help you. I promise." Sophia held his cheek in one hand while the other stayed wrapped around his neck.

"Just stay with me tonight. I can't sleep, I'm exhausted and I just… I can't anymore." Charlie looked into her eyes and a profound sadness was painted across his face.

"Yes. I will, anything." Sophia said. She grabbed her bag and they got into her car and drove away.

Charlie was living with Joey for the time being, but it wasn't permanent. His mother was not recovering as well as the Doctor's had promised she would. If she did not survive her injuries, Charlie would be an orphan. He didn't turn eighteen for another few months, so he had no say in what happened to any of his parent's things or their home. He would be relocated upon the death of his mother, but he had no close relatives. No one was going to take him in. his father had been an only child and his mother's family was estranged long ago. Charlie would be surprised if any of them even showed up to her funeral.

Sophia sent her dad a quick text explaining that she wouldn't be coming home because she was spending the night at Claire's. A lie she hoped he would never discover. He didn't seem to mind, even though it was a school night. She also told Claire where she was and why she ran out of school so fast. Claire, of course, understood and text back saying how she would see her at Joey's later.

They arrived at the house and went down to the finished basement, where Charlie was living temporarily on the pull-out couch. They had it set up to be a second living room and gaming room for Joey and his friends. It was not a horribly dark and spidery basement, but it was a mess. Video game cases were piled high up the side of one wall, there must have been at least fifty games. The controllers were strewn about, with wires in every direction. Charlie's clothes were in various piles around the sofa bed, where he plopped himself down on and looked up at Sophia.

"What do I do now Sophia? What do I do…" he was so defeated, she had no idea how to respond to him.

"You survive somehow. I don't know Charlie, but I'll be here to help you figure it out." She sat beside him and kissed his cheek. Her action snapped him out of a daze and he grabbed her by the waist. They sat there, on the edge of the sofa bed, in the dimly lit basement, and they had their first kiss. He pulled her face towards his, and gently kiss her on the lips. It was a sad kiss. Not a kiss that one dreams of as being their first ever, but it was theirs. Sophia was so thrown by his actions she didn't have time to think about it and kissed him back. It felt wrong and it felt right all at once and it was full of sadness, but also love and acceptance. Where words failed them, they had each other and they had a connection that superseded words. Sophia was falling in love with him, but it felt wrong to be in love when so much was horrible around them.

Charlie wasn't trying to move their relationship along any further. He just needed to feel her, to feel anything other than grief and pain. She gave him a breath of life when he was drowning. She was his relief in the darkness. His light. His red haired, green eyed, beautiful light. Charlie knew they reached the point of no return. She was it for him. She was the one.

They didn't kiss again that night. They talked and held each other and watched a movie. Sophia gave Charlie the escape he needed from his horrifying reality and he was enjoying every second of it.

Eventually Claire and Joey showed up and they all sat in a circle on the sofa bed mattress and talked and laughed and it felt like old times. Charlie was so thankful to have his friends. They were everything to him.

CHAPTER FIFTEEN

A month passed by, and in that time Charlie's mother died. Shortly after her arrival at the hospital she began to have fevers and the doctors discovered internal bleeding. She must have been kicked in the gut before the attackers strangled her. Charlie, with the help of Sophia's dad arranged the funeral for both his parents. A week after her death, Sophia's mother and aunt flew up from North Carolina to attend the funeral and give their condolences to Charlie. Sophia's mother had a hard time understanding how Sophia and Charlie were dating. She laughed at them both the first time they told her, but the connection between Sophia and Charlie became obvious the more time she spent with them. Joey couldn't have Charlie in his house much longer, but his parents agreed that he could stay until school was over.

Another two months passed. Charlie and Sophia spent every day together. Some days were amazing and they went to the ocean, where Sophia would tell Charlie how much better the oceans in North Carolina were. They went to the movies and spent the entire movie holding hands, Sophia's head resting upon Charlie's shoulder.

Other days, however, were not so happy. Charlie often woke in the middle of the night screaming. Sweat pouring down his face, he would scream for mercy and scream for his parents and scream for revenge. As much as he tried to suppress his anger, it was always there. Always hiding beneath the thin surface. The attackers were never found, no trace of them was recovered from the house. They were gone, just like that. They came and they destroyed lives and murdered innocent people and then they left. Just as simply as someone choosing which fruit they prefer at the grocery store. They came and they left and they left a stain on Charlie's heart he could never wash off. He was angry and his anger grew and he was someone he didn't know or understand, unless he was with Sophia.

She was his safety, his peace. She always knew what to say to him and when to say it. They were forced to mature that year, faster than they should have. Charlie had been looking forward to graduation parties and sharing his 'first' drink with his dad, as they sat out on the back patio. He looked forward to telling his mom how unbelievably in love he was with Sophia. All of those hopes and dreams vanished. Taken from him like a slap in the face takes away a man's dignity. Without Sophia around to fill him with joy, he was an empty, angry shell. He put all of his aggression into lifting weights and running as hard and fast as he could. He used to run and lift so he could impress a scout at games. He had always striven to be the strongest and the fastest on the field. His dreams of achieving a football scholarship was now dead just as quickly as his parents died. He was alone and needed a plan for his future if he didn't want to end up on the streets, cup in hand, begging for change.

Charlie came to the conclusion one day, while he was thinking about his upcoming birthday. He would be eighteen in five days and in five days he was going to enroll in the army. It was his only chance. He was strong and fast and smart. He knew joining the army would be easy for him. The only setback to his plan was that he would have to leave Sophia and if he was sent for training and sent overseas, he might never see her again. He thought long and hard about it, even talking about it with Joey and Joey's parents. It was his only logical choice.

Sophia came over after school, just as she always did, and he knew he had to tell her sooner than later. She came in like a breath of fresh air and his courage faltered as he looked upon her smiling face.

"I have to tell you something, and I need you to not get mad." He said to Sophia, as she stepped off the last step into the basement.

"I love how you say hello to me." She said to him. Charlie smiled and grabbed her around the waist and kissed her. She smiled and hugged him and gave him a playful push.

"Is that better?" Charlie asked teasingly.

"Yes. Now what is it?" she said curtly.

"I had to make some hard decisions about my life. I don't know how to say this to you, so I'll just say it and pray to God that you don't hate me," he hesitated, and she fidgeted with the ends of her hair as she watched him, "I'm going to… join the army. I see no other way for me to have a decent life with where I am. My parents are gone, all their money was taken to pay off their bills and mortgage, I have no inheritance. I have no way of going to college and I have no home. I can't live in people's basements my whole life and I want to have a future… with you. How can I provide for you with nothing but the shirt on my back?" he was rambling and he was suddenly on edge. He finished his speech and held his breath. Terrified of what she was going to say.

"Charlie, do you remember that night, that first night we talked, by the pool?" she said. Her question threw him off completely.

"Of course I do. I thought you were going to fall in the pool and drown. Why?" he asked with a nervous laugh.

“You said you would never let me go. I didn’t and couldn’t understand that at the time, but I do now. Charlie, you’re mine and I am yours and I will do and be whatever you need me to. If that means saying goodbye, well it sucks, but I’ll have to say goodbye. Charlie, I… I love you.” She was terrified what this meant for them, but it was right. She had to let him go. She had been thinking about the very same things for a while now. She didn’t want to be the reason he stayed back and stayed in this place where so much sadness had happened. She knew if he really did love her as much as she thought he did, then he would return and they would be fine.

“Sophia, I love you too.” Charlie kissed her, and they kissed with more passion than ever before, and they kissed for minutes on end. He held her, and she held him and they were together in shared sadness and happiness.

CHAPTER SIXTEEN

The next two months happened in a blur for Sophia and Charlie. He began his basic training and was shipped off to Fort Benning in Georgia. Sophia finished high school with Claire and Joey and the three of them spent most of the summer together. Sophia and Charlie talked as much as they could. Through letters and emails and phone calls. Charlie was changing from the high school jock with no ambitions to a respectful and highly motivated soldier. His body changed from lanky teenager to grown, muscular man and his face became darker. He wasn't sure if it was the brutal training each day or the fact that, with every moment he spent away from Sophia, his heart was breaking into pieces, slowly and painfully.

Dealing with his parents' death was proving to be more strenuous than he ever could have imagined. The days before he left for basic, he had his friends with him constantly, distracting him and encouraging him. At basic, he was always surrounded by other people, but he was utterly alone. He could never and would never open up to his fellow soldiers in training about how he felt inside. This constant need to push away feelings to survive drove him to be a bitter and almost heartless man. He returned after his ten-week training period a different person. He was rougher and not as spontaneous. He entered into his hometown with a pain that was visibly stretched across his face.

Joeys home was open to him for his stay, as always. Charlie pulled into the driveway and before his old jeep rolled to a complete stop, a red-haired beauty came bouncing out, ran up to his door, and pulled it open. They stared at each other for a long moment. Sophia taking in all his changes and Charlie left speechless as he noticed she hadn't changed at all. She was beautiful and perfect and more than he could ever deserve. The momet passed as he flung off the seatbelt and grabbed her into his arms. The entire time he was away, all the hard nights holding back angry tears, all the hours spent alone wondering if he should just end his life and make everything go away, they all vanished in the exact second he felt Sophia against him.

"Sophia." Is all he could say, and his entire body gave way. He fell to his knees with her still in his arms and he started to cry. Sophia held him tighter.

"You're okay Charlie, its all okay, I'm here. I love you so much." She said and stroked the back of his freshly shaved head. It was strange seeing him without his shaggy, brown hair curling over the sides of a baseball cap. He looked so much older without it. He had only been gone for ten weeks, but he was clearly a different person.

When he finally wiped away the tears and stood up, he noticed that Joey and Claire had made their way out. He gave them each a hug and Joey grabbed his bag out of the backseat and they all went inside into the basement. Everything felt alarmingly similar to Charlie, like he had never left, and his parents were still alive, and everything was fine.

"I can't go back." He said, startling everyone, "I can't do it. I can't leave again. I thought I could, but I can't." He looked at all their faces and all he could see was more pain.

"Dude, why? What will you do if you don't finish this?" Joey was immediately unimpressed.

"I don't know okay! I can't leave you all again," he looked at Sophia, who was nervously biting her lip and looking from Joey to Charlie, "I can't leave Sophia. It killed me to be away, with only the idea that someday those people will find one of your houses. I still see my dad's face, laying there frozen and dead. It haunts me every single day." This time there were no tears, only anger. Anger Charlie didn't know was possible. His fists were clenched so tightly that his palm began to tear open under his nails. Suddenly, he felt Sophia's hand on his clenched fist, and his fury melted away.

"I'm so sorry Charlie... maybe you two just need some time alone." Said Claire. With that, Claire and Joey got up and went upstairs. Joey patting Charlie on the back as he walked by.

Charlie looked into Sophia's eyes and let out a deep breath.

"I know this is hard for you, but you're here now, please let me help you." Sophia pleaded with him.

He softly took her face into his right hand and with his left he pulled her onto his lap and kissed her. It was deep and gentle, and he held on to that kiss for moments before letting her go. They each took a moment and then they kissed again, and again, and ended up on the pull-out sofa. Sophia gave herself to him for the first time that night and afterwards they lay there in each other's arms until the sun came up. Once Sophia had drifted to sleep, Charlie peeled away from her and got into a hot shower. He stood under the water and thought about his life and Sophia and the army. He had to finish what he started. He had to be the man Sophia deserved, but he didn't want to ever leave her again. His anger would only get worse and the thought of leaving her again killed him inside, but this was his choice.

Charlie left and never looked back. He never questioned what his life would have looked like with Sophia. He never thought about the what-ifs. The moment he came across his mothers' dead body was the moment his life ended.

Made in the USA
Columbia, SC
16 March 2022

57754607R00036